I FEEL WORRIED

By Katie Kawa

Gareth Stevens
Publishing

SOMERSET CO. LIBRARY
BRIDGEWATER, N.J. 08807

Please visit our website, www.garethstevens.com. For a free color catalog of all our high-quality books, call toll free 1-800-542-2595 or fax 1-877-542-2596.

Library of Congress Cataloging-in-Publication Data

Kawa, Katie.
 I feel worried / Katie Kawa.
    p. cm. — (How do I feel?)
 Includes index.
 ISBN 978-1-4339-8128-9 (pbk.)
 ISBN 978-1-4339-8129-6 (6-pack)
 ISBN 978-1-4339-8127-2 (library binding)
 1. Panic attacks—Juvenile literature. 2. Anxiety—Juvenile literature. I. Title.
 RC535.K39 2013
 616.85'223—dc23
                                         2012019209
First Edition

Published in 2013 by
Gareth Stevens Publishing
111 East 14th Street, Suite 349
New York, NY 10003

Copyright © 2013 Gareth Stevens Publishing

Editor: Katie Kawa
Designer: Mickey Harmon

All rights reserved. No part of this book may be reproduced in any form without permission in writing from the publisher, except by a reviewer.

Printed in the United States of America

CPSIA compliance information: Batch #CW13GS For further information contact Gareth Stevens, New York, New York at 1-800-542-2595.

Contents

Today is my first day of school.

I feel worried.
I am worried that
I will not like school.

I am worried that
I will not make friends.

My tummy hurts
when I feel this way.

My mom drives me
to school.
My school is big!

I see my teacher.
Her name is Miss Jones.

I am worried that
she will not be nice.

Miss Jones is very nice!
She is a good teacher.

I meet new friends
at school.
We draw pictures
together.

I do not feel worried anymore.
I love school!

23

Words to Know

picture

teacher

Index

J 616.8522 KAW

Kawa, Katie.

I feel worried 4/13